'What if the lions escape from their cage and chase me up a tree?

'And a branch could snap and I'd land on my back and they'd all start eating me!'

Nick Cope

No I don't wanna do that!

Mum said, 'Hey Joe, well, what do you know? Let's do something nice today.

'We could visit the zoo, yeah just me and you. Hey, what do you say?'

And Joe said...

'So NO, NO, NO, NO,
no I don't wanna do
that.

'Oh NO, NO, NO, NO,
no I don't wanna do
that!'

Mum said, 'OK, look, we've got all day, how about the museum?

'They've got things inside that'll blow your mind, you really have to see 'em.'

And Joe said...

'What if I can't control myself and I have to prod and poke?

'And they lock me away for a year and a day 'cause of all the things I broke?!'

11

'So NO, NO, NO, NO,
no I don't wanna do
that.

'Oh NO, NO, NO, NO,
no I don't wanna do
that!'

'OK,' Mum said, and she scratched her head and she pondered for a bit.

She said, 'We could phone up Pierre who does my hair and he could give your fringe a snip.'

And Joe said...

'What if Pierre just snips and snips and snips it a little bit more?

'There won't be any hair left on my head, it will all be on the floor!'

'So NO, NO, NO, NO,
no I don't wanna do
that.

'Oh NO, NO, NO, NO,
no I don't wanna do
that!'

Mum thought about it and then, quick as a whip, she said, 'I know what we could do.

'We could pop into town and have a look round, we could buy you a new pair of shoes.'

And Joe said...

21

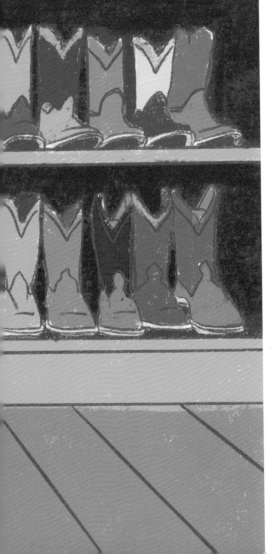

'What if the shoes
are way too big and
they flip and they
flap and they flop?

'Everybody would
be laughing at me as
I hobble around the
shop!'

'So NO, NO, NO, NO,
no I don't wanna do
that.

'Oh NO, NO, NO, NO,
no I don't wanna do
that!'

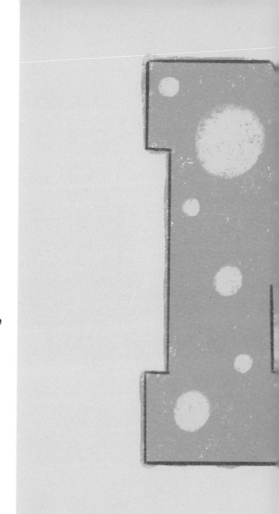

Mum said, 'Hey Joe, well, what do you know? Let's do something really cool!

'The weather looks good so I think that we should head off to the local pool.'

And Joe said...

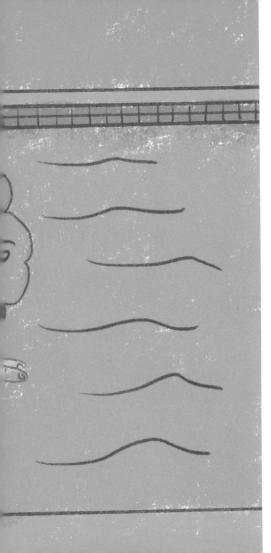

'What if the cord that holds up my shorts is loose and it comes undone?

'How will I know as I swim to and fro that they're all staring at my bum?!'

'So NO, NO, NO, NO,
no I don't wanna do
that.

'Oh NO, NO, NO, NO,
no I don't wanna,
I really don't
wanna,
no I don't wanna
do that!'

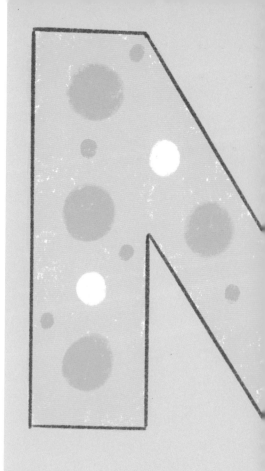

Hey Joe, you've got to let your mother know, it's time for you to make up your mind.

Before it gets too late, there's only so much she can take, the day is nearly done, it's time to decide.

Joe said...

'I guess, what I'd like to do best, would be something really fun.

'I know it's quite late but I think what would be great would be to just stay at home...

'...with my mum!'

Guitar Chords

Over the next few pages you can see where the chords appear in the song, so you can play and sing along.

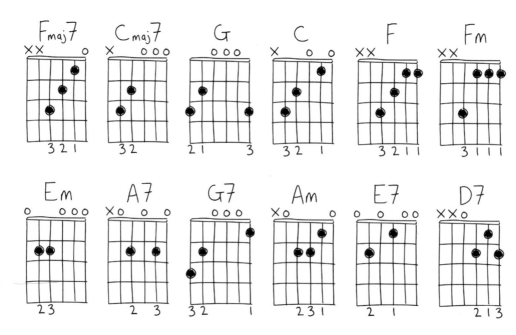

Verse 1

Fmaj7   Cmaj7   Fmaj7   Cmaj7

Mum said, 'Hey Joe, well, what do you know?

Fmaj7   G   C

Let's do something nice today.

Fmaj7 Cmaj7   Fmaj7   Cmaj7

We could visit the zoo, yeah just me and you,

Fmaj7   G   C   F G C

Hey, what do you say?"

Fmaj7   Fm

And Joe said... 'What if the lions escape from their cage and

Em   A7

chase me up a tree?

Fmaj7   Em   Fmaj7   Em

Then a branch could snap and I'd land on my back

Fmaj7   G   C

And they'd all start eating me!'

Chorus

G7   C Am F F
'So   NO, NO, NO, NO,

F   G   C
no I don't wanna do that.

   C Am F F
Oh NO, NO, NO, NO,

F   G   C
no I don't wanna do that!'

Repeat chorus after each verse

On fifth chorus, play the last line as follows:

F   G   Fmaj7
no I don't wanna do that!'

Verse 2

Fmaj7 Cmaj7   Fmaj7 Cmaj7 Fmaj7   G   C
Mum said, 'OK, look, we've got all day, how about the museum?

      Fmaj7 Cmaj7   Fmaj7   Cmaj7
They've got things inside that'll blow your mind,

Fmaj7   G   C   F G C
You really have to see 'em.'

       Fmaj7   Fm   Em
And Joe said... 'What if I can't control myself and I have to prod

   A7
and poke?

    Fmaj7   Em   Fmaj7   Em
And they lock me away for a year and a day,

    Fmaj7 G   C
'cause of all the things I broke?!'

Verse 3

Fmaj7   Cmaj7
'OK,' Mum said,

     Fmaj7   Cmaj7   Fmaj7   G   C
And she scratched her head and she pondered for a bit.

          Fmaj7   Cmaj7   Fmaj7 Cmaj7
She said, 'We could phone up Pierre who does my hair,

    Fmaj7   G   C   F G C
He could give your fringe a snip.'

         Fmaj7   Fm   Em
And Joe said... 'What if Pierre just snips and snips and snips it

    A7
a little bit more?

   Fmaj7 Em   Fmaj7 Em
There won't be any hair left on my head,

   Fmaj7 G   C
It will all be on the floor!'

Verse 4

Fmaj7 Cmaj7 Fmaj7 Cmaj7
Mum thought about it then, quick as a whip,

Fmaj7   G   C
She said, 'I know what we could do.

Fmaj7 Cmaj7 Fmaj7 Cmaj7
We could pop into town and have a look round,

Fmaj7 G   C F G C
We could buy you a new pair of shoes.'

Fmaj7   Fm
And Joe said... 'What if the shoes are way too big,

Em   A7
And they flip and they flap and they flop?

Fmaj7 Em Fmaj7 Em Fmaj7 G   C
Everybody would be laughing at me as I hobble around the shop!'

Verse 5

Fmaj7 Cmaj7   Fmaj7   Cmaj7
Mum said, 'Hey Joe, well, what do you know?

Fmaj7   G   C
Let's do something really cool!

Fmaj7 Cmaj7   Fmaj7   Cmaj7
The weather looks good so I think that we should,

Fmaj7 G C   F G C
Head off to the local pool.'

Fmaj7   Fm   Em
And Joe said... 'What if the cord that holds up my shorts is loose

A7
and it comes undone?

Fmaj7 Em   Fmaj7   Em
How will I know as I swim to and fro,

Fmaj7   G   C
That they're all staring at my bum?!'

Middle Eight

Fmaj7   Cmaj7

Hey Joe, you've got to let your mother know,

Fmaj7   Em

It's time for you to make up your mind,

      Fmaj7   E7

Before it gets too late, there's only so much she can take,

   F   D7

The day is nearly done, it's time to decide...

  Fmaj7   Cmaj7   Fmaj7 Cmaj7

Joe said, 'I guess, what I'd like to do best,

      Fmaj7   G   C

would be something really fun,

 Fmaj7   Cmaj7   Fmaj7   Cmaj7

I know it's quite late but I think what would be great would be to

Fmaj7   G   C

just stay at home with my mum!'

Nick Cope

Nick writes songs for young children and regularly performs at schools, theatres, festivals and events for families around the country. He has established a strong following all over the world, with both parents and children loving his work. In a previous life, Nick was the lead singer of the rock band The Candyskins.
Nick's songs are on
iTunes and YouTube.
www.nickcope.co.uk

Books in the series

Why is the sky blue?
Author Nick Cope
ISBN 9781912213528
Published by Graffeg

Books in the series

The very silly dog

Author Nick Cope

ISBN 9781912213511

Published by Graffeg